GRANDPA MUDCAKE *and the* Rickety Robot

Written and Illustrated by Sophia J. Ferguson

For Max

First published in Great Britain 2021 by Macnaughtan Books
Text and illustration copyright © Sophia J. Ferguson

ISBN: 978-1-914523-03-8

You may not know this, but Grandpa Mudcake likes to make things.

At the bottom of his garden is a shed.

Inside the shed, he has lots of tools.

There are hammers, saws, screwdrivers, nails and lots of bits of metal and wood.

Can you guess what Grandpa is making in his shed today?

Grandpa is making a robot.

He's been making it for a VERY long time.

At last, the robot is finished.

Grandpa wants to show it to his grandson, Little Jimmy.

Little Jimmy is coming to stay for the weekend.

Suddenly, there's a loud knock on the shed door.

Little Jimmy has arrived.

"Let me in Grandpa!" he shouts.

"WOW!" gasps Little Jimmy when he sees the robot.

"What's the robot for?" he asks Grandpa.

"The robot's going to help me with lots of jobs" replies Grandpa.

"I want to see him move" says Little Jimmy, excitedly.

"First, help me oil his wheels" says Grandpa.

Little Jimmy squirts some oil from the oil can onto the robot's wheels.

"Good, now we can test him" says Grandpa.

Grandpa carefully carries the robot into the garden.

"Grandpa, the robot doesn't have a face" says Little Jimmy.

"Perhaps you could draw one later and we can glue it on" suggests Grandpa.

Grandpa switches the robot on.

The robot makes a loud, clunkety noise.

Grandpa presses "FORWARD" on the remote control.

Slowly, the robot rattles and squeaks along the grass.

Then, SUDDENLY, it lurches forward.

"Oh no!" shouts Little Jimmy.

The robot has fallen flat on its face.

One arm and a leg have fallen off.

"Oh dear" sighs Grandpa, "It's too rickety."

"What does rickety mean?" asks Little Jimmy.

"It means wobbly" replies Grandpa.

"Why don't you go and draw a face for the robot with Grandma" says Grandpa, "I need to put the robot back together."

Little Jimmy runs into the house.

Grandma fetches some paper and pens.

Little Jimmy draws a big mouth and some big eyes.

By evening, Grandpa has fixed the robot.

He helps Little Jimmy glue on the robot's face.

"He's a real robot now" says Little Jimmy.

"His name is Robert, the Rickety Robot!" he laughs.

"That's a good name" says Grandpa, "We'll test Robert again tomorrow" he adds.

The next day, Grandpa takes Robert into the street.
Some people stop by to watch.
Grandpa presses "FORWARD" on the remote control.
Slowly, Robert wobbles along the street.
Then, with a big lurch, he disappears around the corner.
Grandpa desperately tries to turn Robert back.
"Oh dear, I think he's fallen over" he panics.
But, to Grandpa's delight, Robert suddenly
reappears and rattles back along the street.
Everyone claps and cheers.

"Let's see if Robert can carry my golf clubs round the golf course," Grandpa says later that day.
Grandpa, Little Jimmy, and Robert set off in the car.
At the golf course, Grandpa hangs his heavy golf bag over Robert's shoulder.
Robert carries the clubs round the WHOLE golf course without falling over.
But his wheels have made HUGE muddy lines ALL over the grass.
Grandpa is told NEVER to bring his robot to the golf course again!

On the way home, Grandpa stops at the DIY store.
"I need to buy a new hammer and some glue"
he says, "Let's see if Robert can push the
shopping trolley."
Grandpa helps Little Jimmy into the trolley.
They all head into the store.
At first, Robert pushes the trolley very well.
Then, SUDDENLY, he lurches forward.

"Oh help!" gasps Grandpa.

Robert ZOOMS into the gardening section and knocks over four pot plants and some gardening tools.

Grandpa is told NEVER to bring his robot to the DIY store again!

"Oh dear" says Grandpa to Little Jimmy when they arrive home, "There must be something Robert can help us with. We'll try again tomorrow," he sighs.

"Let's see if Robert can cut the grass" says Grandpa the next morning.

Grandpa attaches Robert's arms to the lawnmower.

Sheena and her cat, Derek, who live next door, have come to watch over the garden fence.

Robert cuts a long strip of grass very neatly.

But just as Robert turns, he lurches forward and crashes into the garden fence.

Robert now has a big dent on his head.

It's been a tiring weekend testing Robert.

After lunch, Grandpa and Little Jimmy fall fast asleep.

They're woken a bit later by Grandma.

"Would you like some cake?" she calls from the kitchen.

"Let's see if Robert can fetch the cake" Grandpa says to Little Jimmy.

Using the remote control, Grandpa directs Robert out of the sitting room, along the hall, and towards the kitchen.

Little Jimmy follows Robert into the kitchen.

"Robert's going to carry the cake," he tells Grandma.

"I hope he doesn't drop it!" she laughs.

Grandma places a tray across Robert's arms.

On the tray, she puts two slices of cake.

"He's ready" Little Jimmy shouts to Grandpa.

Grandpa directs Robert back to the sitting room.

Robert arrives safely WITHOUT falling over.

"Thank you, Robert" smiles Grandpa as he bites into his cake, "At last we've found a job you can do!"

It's time for Little Jimmy to go home.
"Can Robert do something funny?" he asks Grandpa.
Grandpa starts pressing the remote control.
Suddenly, Robert's head spins around three times.
Then Robert bends over, picks up Little Jimmy's teddy and throws it into the air.
The teddy lands on top of Little Jimmy's head!
Little Jimmy and Grandpa laugh out loud.
"I'll do some more work on Robert," says Grandpa, "And next time you visit, he'll be a bit less rickety."
Little Jimmy can't wait to see Robert again.

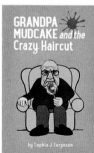

GRANDPA MUDCAKE *and the* Crazy Haircut

by Sophia J Ferguson

GRANDPA MUDCAKE *and the* Crazy Tea Party

by Sophia J Ferguson

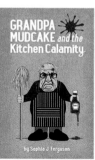

GRANDPA MUDCAKE *and the* Kitchen Calamity

by Sophia J Ferguson

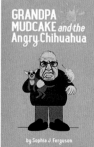

GRANDPA MUDCAKE *and the* Angry Chihuahua

by Sophia J. Ferguson

GRANDPA MUDCAKE *goes* Internet Shopping

by Sophia J Ferguson

GRANDPA MUDCAKE *and the* Rickety Robot

by Sophia J Ferguson

GRANDPA MUDCAKE *and the* Nosey Chicken

by Sophia J Ferguson

GRANDPA MUDCAKE *goes to* The Gym

by Sophia J Ferguson

The HANDY GADGET *Catalogue*

A Grandpa Mudcake SPECIAL EDITION
by Sophia J. Ferguson

THE REGINALD STINKBOTTOM COLOURING BOOK

THE ADVENTURES OF REGINALD STINKBOTTOM

GRANDPA MUDCAKE.com

Made in the USA
Middletown, DE
15 December 2022

18832366R00020